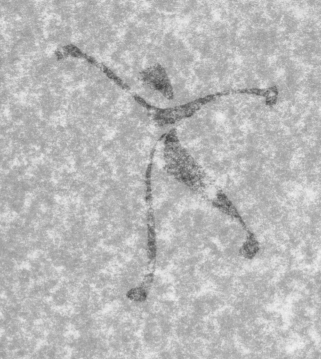

A Cry from the Clay

Books by Esther Bender

Lemon Tree Series
Katie and the Lemon Tree
Virginia and the Tiny One

Picture Storybooks
April Bluebird
The Crooked Tree
Search for a Fawn

Mystery
Shadow at Sun Lake

Meditations
A Cry from the Clay

Toll-free book ordering:
1-800-759-4447

Study Guides for The Crooked Tree
and Search for a Fawn
Ordering address:
PO Box 732, Grantsville, MD 21536

A Cry from the Clay

Esther Bender

Herald
Press

Scottdale, Pennsylvania
Waterloo, Ontario

01036 1524

Library of Congress Cataloging–in-Publication Data

Bender, Esther, 1942-
    A cry from the clay / Esther Bender.
        p.   cm.
    ISBN 0-8361-9100-5 (alk. paper)
    I. Title.
PS3552.E53848C79   1999
811'.54—dc21   98-45527

The paper used in this publication is recycled and meets the mini-
mum requirements of the American National Standard for Information Sciences—Permanence of Paper for Printed Library Materials,
ANSI Z39.48-1984.

A CRY FROM THE CLAY
Copyright © 1999 by Herald Press, Scottdale, Pa. 15683
    Published simultaneously in Canada by Herald Press,
    Waterloo, Ont. N2L 6H7. All rights reserved
Library of Congress Catalog Card Number: 98-45527
International Standard Book Number: 0-8361-9100-5
Printed in the United States of America
Photographs, images, and cover photo by Esther Bender
All pottery by Lynn Lais
Book and cover design by Gwen M. Stamm

08 07 06 05 04 03 02 01 00 99 10 9 8 7 6 5 4 3 2 1

To Dad, with love

O Lord,
you are our Father.
We are the clay,
and you are our Potter.
We are all the work
of your hand.

—Isaiah 64:8, adapted

Contents

*All pottery by
Lynn Lais*

Lynn Lais is the potter in residence at Spruce Forest Artisan Village near Grantsville, Maryland. He has been a self-employed studio artist since 1981. He lives nearby with his wife, Jan, and two children.

Lais was born in Portland, Oregon, and grew up in Hesston, Kansas. He holds an Associate Degree from Hesston College and a B.A. in art from Goshen (Indiana) College. He attended Wichita State University for graduate studies.

Following graduation in 1978, Lais went to Europe for three years, working as a journeyman in Belgium and Switzerland. While there, he refined his skills and acquired new decorating techniques.

Every year, Lais produces several thousand unique pieces. Each pot is individually formed, decorated, glazed with lead-free glazes, and fired in a kiln. The pottery may be used in an oven or microwave and is dishwasher safe.

He makes each piece with care and designs it to work well. A genuine Lais piece will have the Lais signature (shown under his photo) on the bottom of the pottery.

Readers may contact the artist at 199 Casselman Road, Grantsville, MD 21536 (301-895-5932).

*All text, photos,
and images
by Esther Bender*

The author, Esther Bender, lives near Grantsville, Maryland, with her husband, Jason. They have five grown daughters. Now retired, she was a teacher for twenty-three years. Since 1978 she has struggled with Parkinson's disease.

Bender is a graduate of Frostburg State University and earned a master's degree in elementary education.

She took courses in writing and has published many articles and books (see page 2). She is a member of the Society of Children's Book Writers and Illustrators.

Bender grew up in Springs, Pennsylvania, and was active in the Springs Mennonite Church. Now she and her husband are members of First Presbyterian Church, Cumberland.

Readers may contact the author at PO Box 732, Grantsville, MD 21536 (301-895-5736).

"Help, Lord!"

All on earth

cry to the Potter

someday, some way.

The Master Potter

Here is another message . . .
from the Lord:
"Go down to the shop
where clay pots and jars are made
and I will talk to you there."

I did as he told me,
and found the potter
working at his wheel.
But the jar that he was forming
didn't turn out as he wished,
so he kneaded it into a lump
and started again.

Then the Lord said: . . .
"Can't I do to you
as this potter has done
to his clay?
As the clay is
in the potter's hand,
so are you in my hand."

(Jeremiah 18:1-6, LB)

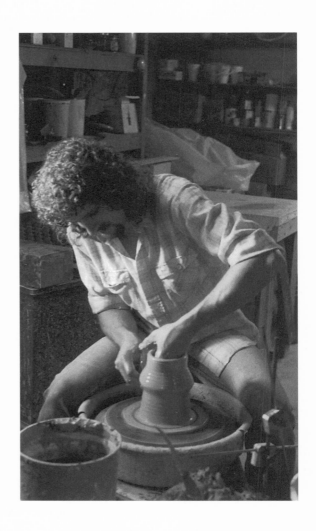

**We are the clay, and
you are our Potter.
We are all the work
of your hand.**
—Isaiah 64:8

The Clay

I, a lump of clay!
The Lord, Creator, Potter!
God kneaded me
and placed me
on this wheel,
the spinning
planet earth.
I was content
to be just me.

But now
the Potter
wants me,
needs me,
crushes me,
rewets, rekneads my clay.
On the wheel, a new form grows.

It has been said
that form must follow function.
Not so, the way the Potter works.
He whispers of functions
that he has in mind for me.

This clay,
when pushed in here,
will move out there,
searching, seeking,
until I find the function
this new form demands.

We are the clay, and
you are our Potter.
We are all the work
of your hand.
—*Isaiah 64:8*

Buckets of Mud

Buckets of clay! Mud!
Infinite potential!

What will the artist make?

Slabs of clay cut into tiles to walk on.
Tiny geometric shapes for a mosaic.

Ornamental bowls.
Ceramic dish with cover, duck for a handle.

Cake plate with a foot.
Roaster with words carved in the top.
Large rectangular flat tray.

Figures and figurines.
Beautiful ladies, handsome men, funny clowns.
A small wistful boy.
Doll faces, arms, and legs.

Pots to hold light.
Bowl with holes to set a candle in.
Round lamps with a ball and wick.

Dinner plates.
Teapots, cups, and saucers,
delicate and light
or thick and heavy.

Each artist has a specialty.
So too the Potter.
His specialty is living clay,
made with a secret formula.

He made a myriad of animals.
And when he'd finished them,
he made his crowning work of art—
the human body.

**Within a child lies
the most awesome
potential in the
whole universe.**

Decorating

A potter would do only half a job
if he skipped the glazing
and the decorating.
Unless he wanted unglazed clay
for water to seep through,
as in the making of a flowerpot
or terra-cotta statues for a garden.

He who would hold water in his art,
must glaze and decorate.
He develops a unique style,
the hallmark of his work.
With brush or dipping, he adds color.
With stylus or a brush, a signature
that claims his art,
forever his,
although it may be owned by many.

The artist's style evolves.
Long after he is dead,
collectors talk of early work and late.
The artist pushes to excel,
one piece above another,
and over time
emerges a pattern
of design and decoration.
Well-made pieces gain in value
as pieces break.
His pottery grows scarce.

This potter has a hand that's free.
A line around the top, then falling swirls
in flowerlike cascade, as though a lilac
drooped its head and then curled up.
There are no flowers in his work,
no animals, no plants, or trees.
But there is rhythm and there's grace,
pure designs that please
and hold attention.

That's the way the Master Potter decorates,
with motion and with rhythm,
and a swirl that is a face.

On the body, each
person bears the
Creator's signature.

Conversation

The clay said, "Lord, you are perfect.
Why did you make me defective?"

And the Lord said,
"You, too, are perfect—
for my purpose!"

"What purpose?" asked the clay.

"For dropping crumbs!"

"Crumbs!
You made me to drop crumbs?"

"Have you not heard
that I feed the puppies
with crumbs
from the rich man's table?
I have made you to drop crumbs."

"Lord, why not make me perfect?
Then I could carry
whole loaves of bread?"

"Will you not trust me?
I am perfect.
I did not make you
to carry whole loaves."

"Why?"

"Few will eat whole loaves,
but many will eat crumbs.
I made you to drop crumbs.
The crumbs are crumbs
of the Bread of Life,
and crumbs are enough for puppies."

"Then, Lord, give me lots of crumbs."

"I will give them to you as you need them,
and you will not even know
when you drop them."

**Anyone eating this
Bread shall live forever.**
—John 6:51, LB

Writing is the making

of a stew

that simmers in the mind

long after pen

is lifted from the paper.

Not Poetry!
Not Artistry!

This is not poetry—
this arrangement of my words
upon the page.
I know nothing of poetry.

These are ideas and stories
I am hearing in my head,
symphony of sounds
and tempos intertwining,
advancing and retreating,
clashing loudly,
falling to a whisper.

These are images and pictures
I am seeing in my head,
collage of clippings
and textures interwoven,
bright and shiny,
sometimes mellow,
velvety as peach fuzz.

This is not artistry—
this making images
with camera and computer.
I know nothing of artistry.
These are arrangements.

THIS IS FUN!

Satisfy us, . . . so that
we may rejoice and
be glad all our days.
—Psalm 90:14

Write Mishmash!

Write along with me.
I invite you to write mishmash!

I once wrote diary.
No more.
Now I am free!
I write mishmash!
Joyfully write mishmash!

Stories, copied Scriptures,
lists and phrases,
quotations from a speaker on TV,
prayers and goals,
sentence fragments!
I write free!

Mishmash contains my prayers:
"Help, Lord!
Help me control my body
for just one hour tomorrow."
Later: "Thank you, Lord!"

Mishmash contains my goals,
dreams, and emotions,
the raw stuff of stories.

Do you too want to be free?
Write along with me.
Write mishmash!

O Lord, . . . you have
loosed my bonds.
—*Psalm 116:16*

Was, and Is, and Will Be!

The trillium bears the message of the three,
not the holy Trinity,
but was, and is, and will be.
The past, the present, and the future
hold all there is to write about.

The past may be regarded as dead history.
Beyond our life, in past or in the future,
all knowledge that we have of time is words.
Beyond our life, there is no memory.

I will not be superior in my looking
to the future.
How do I know it will be bright and fine?
I will not glorify the past.
How do I know it was as I believe?

Past, present, future:
God has no need for these inventions.
They are just words, words, words.
But . . .
    it was no mistake that God is called
        The Author.
He knew that to communicate with us
he would need words.

I will not disdain the writing down
of words.
I will follow in the footsteps
of The Author.

I pick my tense in writing.
Makes no difference.
All there is to write about
is there in . . .
    was, and is, and will be.

Humans, Creators!

When humans found clay,
perhaps along a riverbed,
and shaped it into bowls
to carry nuts and berries or dry seeds,
the rain would melt the bowls
to mud.

But then, humans shaped a bowl,
put food in it,
and cooked it over fire.
Ah-ha!
The fire had made the bowl
turn hard as rock.
Better than drying in the sun.

And now,
humans yearned for beauty.
They painted on the bowls
with colored clays,
used sticks to imprint it,
and pressed into its surface
textures of many kinds.
Then they fired the bowls,
with purpose.

Bowls with high sides
made pitchers.
Lids made rodent-safe containers.

Why this urge to shape more skillfully?
To paint, to glaze?
And to display them on a shelf?

The Creator
made us in his image.
Creating—what common folks require
to feel fulfilled.

The baby eagerly creates.
Left to herself,
she plays in mud.
Later, shapes it into bowls
without instruction.
Lets it harden in the sun.

Ancient art, infant art!
Humans in the Creator's image!

I would create.
Not in mud or pottery,
but words.

All would create
or be as dry bones,
rattling in the wind.

**When God created
humans, he made them
in the likeness of God.
—*Genesis 5:1, adapted***

"Write!" Said the Lord

I asked to be healed.
The Lord said, "Write!"

"Why must I write?" I asked.

"Write so you will know
what you truly want and need.
Then ask for it.

"Write so you will remember
what you asked
and so you will know, someday,
that I answered."

I began to write:
June 1, 1992—Copying from the Bible
is a task I give myself
because I'm a visual, tactile learner.

Soon I saw the value of writing:
June 3, 1992—Now, Lord, it's 1992.
I'd like to have a book accepted soon.
Please.

June 8, 1992—Dear God,
Why do I think about you,
and ask your help, then promptly forget
what I wanted help with?
(That's why I need to write prayers.)

February 4, 1993—O Provider,
I began this journal with prayer
for the sale of a book.
Eight months later, you did it.
The letter came from Herald Press,
accepting *Katie and the Lemon Tree*.
(When I write down prayers,
I begin to see when and how
God answers them.)

May 2, 1993—Lord, I'm depending on you
for the vision, the shape of the future.
I want to inspire, to write, create!

May 30, 1993—Today my husband, Jason, said,
"The act of writing enters a thought
into your subconscious.
It stays there and can't be pulled out,
but continues to affect you for time to come."

**God answers prayer?
Prove it! Write down
prayers and answers!**

Writing about my disability

is the peeling of an onion,

hidden layer after layer,

while I weep,

until there is nothing more

to cry about.

My onion is Parkinson's.

What Is Parkinson's?

Parkinson's disease is a degenerative disorder of the brain that affects control of body movement. Symptoms appear when about 80 percent of the cells in the substantia nigra region of the brain quit functioning.

Tremor is only one of many symptoms. Others are slowness, stiffness, stooped posture, soft voice, facial stare, shuffling walk, loss of balance, and small illegible writing. These symptoms and others occur together in varying combinations of intensity in individual people. Together they are known as the Parkinson's syndrome.

Although Parkinson's appears to be a disturbance of the muscles, the disease is in the brain, which controls the speed and fluidity of muscle movement. The brain is like a computer with millions of circuits. In normal people, cells transmit impulses by release of a chemical called dopamine.

Dopamine is one of many chemicals, all called neurotransmitters, which control body action. When brain cells are unable to produce adequate amounts of dopamine, store it, and release it, the impaired movements of Parkinson's are seen.

Most people with this disease become aware of it at a specific time and place. Yet it has likely been developing for years before it is noticed.

Parkinson's is a progressive disease. It begins insidiously and worsens with time, although the rate of progression varies from person to person. It most commonly begins between ages fifty and seventy, but it can begin much earlier or later.

The causes and a cure for Parkinson's are still elusive, but research is yielding promising results. For years, treatment has consisted of giving medication, levodopa, to partially replace the dopamine needed by the brain. True dopamine cannot be given because the blood-brain barrier, meant to protect the brain, will not let dopamine pass into the brain cells. The taking of levodopa for Parkinson's is the equivalent of taking insulin for blood-sugar problems.

Today, Sinemet, consisting of levodopa-carbidopa, remains the primary drug for treating Parkinson's. There are many new drug combinations aimed at balancing chemicals in the brain. Since optimal results may depend on four or five drugs, a Parkinson's patient may seem to be a "pill popper." As the insulin-dependent must snack to maintain blood-sugar levels, so the dopamine dependent must "snack" on pills.

Parkinson's patients often feel as though they are becoming paralyzed. When the dopamine level is low, the body feels as though one were trying to move an ocean liner with one small tugboat. Speech is suppressed, and so is smiling. This makes Parkinson's patients sometimes appear to be unfriendly. While outwardly controlled, they may feel as though they are trembling inside and would lose control of both body and emotions if they relaxed.

Parkinson's can be devastating to families who care for a loved one through many years of disability and increasing helplessness. Hope and pray that a cure may soon be found for this disease.

—*Verified by Dr. Howard Weiss*
 Sinai Hospital, Baltimore

Parkinson's slowly withers the body and its ability to respond.

As an Acorn

When an oak tree grows,
it doesn't come full-leafed and tall,
but as an acorn,
starting small and pushing
from the inside out,
until
a tree has formed.

When disease grows,
it doesn't come, its form complete,
but as an acorn,
starting small and pushing
from the inside out,
until
its symptoms show it's there.

I saw the acorn splitting
when I said,
"My hand is stuttering today.
See! When I write,
my hand makes backward jerks."

I saw the roots go down
when I saw myself
mirrored in a store window,
bent forward from the hips,
like an adjustable straw
in a glass of soda.
I was dismayed!
"Stand up straight!"
I told myself.

I saw a shoot come out
when I worked the counter
of our restaurant.
I was tired and shaky.
Then a man, his fingers shaking,
told me,
"This whiskey is my medicine
for Parkinson's."
I thought, *Oh, yea-uh?*
I did not know
the shoot was mine,
as well as his.

**The disease process
starts long before
disease is visible.**

Parkinson's Came Nibbling

Parkinson's came nibbling,
quiet as a gray squirrel,
determined as a caterpillar
munching milkweed leaves.

I was reading a story
to twenty-four small students,
seated around me on the floor.
Suddenly, I had a munching feeling
in the left side of my head
and a jerk of my right leg.
I laughed!

"Why are you laughing, Teacher?"

"My leg jerked by itself!"

Another munching and a jerk!

"I saw it!"
"I saw your leg jerk!"
Twenty-four pairs of wide, curious eyes
faced me.

"It's nothing," I said.
"Let's read!"

There was no more nibbling.
But when I wrote, my left foot contracted.

"Are you going to the doctor?"
asked my family.

"What would I tell the doctor?
That I had a funny feeling in my head?"

To myself, I said,
"Wait and see.
It will all go away.
I'll never be able to say
what caused it."

It went away—
that munching feeling—
but my hand and my leg
seemed to be fused together.
Neither worked
without involving the other.

**Parkinson's may
develop for ten or more
years before the first
symptoms are noticed.**

The Hummingbird

Why does this hummingbird tremble?
It flew into the window,
and now it trembles.

"Why do I shake?
Mother, can you see my hands are shaking?"

"Yes, I see your hands are shaking.
Shaking hands are in the family.
Your great-uncle Bob shook so much
he wouldn't eat at a table with others."

"But I'm not old like my great-uncle Bob.
I'm only thirty-five!"

"Well, shaking's in the family.
Your great-aunt Emma had Parkinson's.
She shook all the time."

Great-aunt Emma in a wheelchair, trembling.
Parkinson's disease!
A name for it, at last!

I sought medical advice:
"Doctor, sometimes my hands shake
and I feel trembly inside."

"I don't see any trembling.
Everyone shakes.
See, I can make my body shake."

The doctor stiffened his body
until he shook.
Then he said, "It's nothing."

It's probably nothing,
I repeated to myself.
Probably nothing.
Probably nothing.
Then why must I keep repeating
while my insides crumble?

In the deepest part of me,
I knew the truth.

The hummingbird sits for a time
in kind hands.
Then it flies away.

I repeated, repeated:
Probably nothing.
Probably nothing.
Probably nothing.

Parkinson's unbalances
body chemicals;
shock unbalanced
the chemicals in
the hummingbird.

Sunlight and Shadow

Sunlight on the clay:
"Now I know it's Parkinson's."
The local doctor made a diagnosis.
I was relieved to know:
"Very mild Parkinson's.
May not be disabling for thirty years.
No medication needed."

Yet . . . shadows on the clay:
"May be disabling in five years."

At home I wondered:
What is Parkinson's?

The need to know was there.
I asked. I read.
The shadow shifted
and changed in size and shape.

My body changed.
I went out walking every day,
click, clump, click, clump, click, clump.
Right-sided Parkinson's
made me walk unevenly.
Cog-wheeling, it's called.

I was tired, so tired.
My writing was getting smaller.
I could no longer type with ten fingers.
I trembled.
The shadow shifted
and changed in size and shape.

Is this really Parkinson's?

I went to Johns Hopkins Hospital.
Diagnosis: "Parkinson's."

"Medication needed."

**Proud mortal!
Frail as breath!
A shadow!**
*—Psalm 39:5-6, LB,
  adapted*

Exoskin

Why this shaking of my hands?
An inheritance from my father's father?

I was a tiny girl when I knelt beside him
as he set out strawberry plants.
His hands were stiff and veined,
his movements slow.
"Grandpa, why do you shake?"

"Rheumatism," he said.
The sky was gray and cold.
I wanted to make him better.

"Let's go in, Grandpa,
where it's warm."

"A few more plants," he said.
I waited with impatience.

Inside, in the warmth and light,
I was pleased I'd cared for Grandpa.
Soon after that, Grandpa died.

Did he have Parkinson's?
Did I get it
from my mother and my father?
Is death the shedding of a skin,
an exoskin and not an exoskeleton,
the forsaking of a worn-out body?

Until then, I will enjoy:
September 13, 1993
Thank you, Lord, for this beautiful night, the
sounds of insects singing in the grass. It is a night
to make me love the earth—rich, humus scent, the
smell of bark, small tree frogs singing.

February 20, 1998
What if all the insects
mourned over the exoskeletons
of their comrades who passed
on? Imagine the singing in
the grass!

Help, Lord!

Help, Lord!
I have Parkinson's.
Please don't let this disease progress.

I want to be a wife
and a friend and lover,
as on our honeymoon.
When our car broke down,
I wheeled us down Cape Hatteras
in that old Rent-a-Wreck,
rusted, no paint left, no third gear.
The wind blew my hair
and that white floppy hat!
The sun was in our laughter,
the ocean in our ears.
Our car broke down—what a blessing!

We had an extra week of honeymoon.
We laughed and laughed!
But now this is no laughing matter.
I don't want to lose my laughing face
for the stiff mask of Parkinson's.

I don't want to lose
my freedom to drive,
my freedom to walk,
the alertness of my mind,
and the wit to argue and debate.
We've always loved debate, you know.
Remember, Lord,
how we missed our exit
on the Pennsylvania Turnpike?
We had to drive thirty miles to the next one,
all because we were talking.

I want to go on talking,
laughing, being.
I want to run up steps,
drive alone to town,
and drive around the lake
on Sunday afternoons.

I want to be heard
without being breathless
or not understood.

Help, Lord!
I want to stay just as I am.
Don't let this disease progress!

**Trust in the Lord
with all your heart,
and do not rely on
your own insight.**
—Proverbs 3:5

Mayo Clinic

We left home for Mayo Clinic,
hopeful that Parkinson's wasn't Parkinson's.
We had heard there was a chance. . . .

As we neared Rochester, Minnesota,
there were thunderclouds up ahead,
piled high and black,
brooding over the plain.

Rain began pounding, lightning flashing,
crashing all around us.
Windshield wipers were
clapping without joy,
applauding my arrival.

Is this real?
Or am I an actress in a play?

A sudden break above!
A hole torn in the heavens!

Streams of light
turned trees green velvet,
tipped with gold.
A rainbow touched earth to earth.

My sign! My symbol!
God cares for me!
Whatever happens will be right!

Three days later—
a diagnosis: Parkinson's.
But I learned more. The doctors said,
"There is no magic healing.
Your body is yours to care for.
No one else cares about it as you do!
Observe it! Study it!
Keep records about it.
Try changes in lifestyle."

We left Rochester.

I am not an actress in a play.
I am real!
God cares for me!

I remember not a diagnosis,
but joy and a rainbow.
I came home and began a diary,
recording information I have needed
many times since.

**Those who are attentive
to a matter will prosper.**
—*Proverbs 16:20*

Toes Curl Under

Fifteen miles from home,
I reached into my purse.
My pills weren't there.

I should go home immediately,
but I need to buy a birthday present.
I can do that quickly.

On my way to pay at the checkout,
my toes ached.
Then my feet stuck to the floor.
My toes curled under.
I held onto a shelf.

My brain is out of dopamine.
Brain circuits are electrical.
The switch is OFF.
So this is the on-off of Parkinson's.
Help, Lord!

"What's wrong, lady?"
a man asked me.

"I forgot my medication."

"I'll check out for you," he said.

Suddenly, my toes uncurled.
I checked out.
The clerk carried out my package.

Beside the car, my toes curled under.

My switch is OFF again.
No dimmer switch!

The clerk unlocked the car
and put the gift inside.
He handed me the keys.
"Shall I call the rescue squad?"

"No, it's only my walking."
"I'll be okay when I sit down."

He was concerned.

Then the ON.

I got into the car.
I drove straight home, with no more trouble.

But now I knew what "freezing" meant.

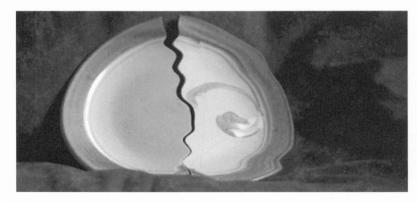

It's hard to admit that
you need help.
Let others assist
as needed.

The Kneading Process

Kneading! Reworking of the clay.
Sometimes a painful process!

Christmas 1995.
For two days,
the doctor withdrew all drugs,
then put me in the hospital
to adjust my medications.
I wasn't prepared for the severity
of disease without medications.
My body couldn't seem to recover
or adjust to new time-release drugs.

I came home from the hospital
in unstable condition.
Paralysis overcame me
several times a day.
I was full of fear.
I could not stay alone
because I had no warning
when paralysis would come.
One minute, walking.
The next minute, paralyzed.

Then I couldn't reach my pills
to break the downward spiral.
By day, my mother and my father
cared for me.
By night, my husband cared for me.

Lord, I didn't know
that you were kneading me.

Now I know
you were answering my prayers,
preparing me to leave this town,
to seek help elsewhere.
Now I know
you planned for a pallidotomy—
surgery for Parkinson's.

A pallidotomy!
It gave me back my self-control!
My social life!
My calmness, my joy!

I never thought
that I'd be grateful
for such a frightening time,
but I am.

Thank you,
Lord!

Thank you,
Lord!

Thank you,
Lord!"

Often we delay our action, lacking a solution, till God provides direction.

The Pallidotomy

Johns Hopkins Hospital, Baltimore.
Electric drill, screwdrivers in a box.
The doctor said, "Hold these."
He plopped them on the stretcher
where I lay, my head shaved
down the middle.
I would have my "frames" put on.

Once fearful, now unafraid,
last night I'd given fear to God.
He sent a loving Presence
and a peace—
with a spirit of adventure!

Frames to immobilize my head.
With a needle
they numbed four spots,
two behind my ears,
two on my forehead,
Drill roared into skull.
Screws turned in the drill holes.
My frames were on.

Time for surgery.
The surgeon said,
"This needle will numb your skin.
After that—the brain feels no pain."
The drill bit bone, whined,
abruptly wound down
as it went through.

Two men watched a scanner beside me
as the surgeon inserted probes in my head.

The surgeon moved my arm.
I heard a squeaking sound,
a sound like window-washing.
Then he said,
"Now shut your eyes.
Look for the shower of light.
That will mean we are very close
to your center of vision."
I shut my eyes and was not afraid.
The loving Presence was beside me.

I didn't want to lose my sight.
I would concentrate.
Then I saw the shower of light,
fireworks of the brain,
a mental Fourth of July.
I put up my hand to let them know
I saw it.

Again and again, I announced the light.
At last, my brain was mapped,
not once, but several times.
There would be no second chances.
The coordinates were checked
and rechecked.
There were two clusters of cells
to be destroyed.

**Do not let your hearts
be troubled.**
—John 14:27

Pray for confidence.

The "burning" process began.
I felt my body stretching, relaxing.
My face began to smile.
It's working! I can feel it working!
Thank you, Lord!

After surgery,
my loving family stood around me.
"Mom, you're smiling
like you haven't smiled in years!"
I saw excitement in their faces.

When all had gone home,
I took out my diary
and read what I had written
the night before:

Tomorrow, we are on an adventure,
my doctor, my God, and I. . . .
Deep in the forest of brain cells,
where messages once swung free,
now clogged with dead wood and thicket,
my doctor will prune for me.
Then I'll be the one with treasure,
richer time to be lived in good measure.
Having glimpsed a world few living will see,
I'll come home from my adventure
in technology.
My doctor, my God, and me.

I had come safely home
with a miracle—no, two miracles:
the surgery and the peace!

After a patient has had Parkinson's for several years, brain receptors become supersensitive to fluctuating dopamine levels. A garbling of information causes jerking, writhing motions or periods of marked immobility. When alternate pathway(s) are surgically interrupted, the brain can again respond more reliably to medication.

—Explanation by Dr. Howard Weiss,
   Sinai Hospital, Baltimore
—Surgery by Dr. Frederick Lenz,
   John Hopkins Hospital, Baltimore

My peace I give to you.
—John 14:27

A Future with Parkinson's

I don't want to think
beyond this age and stage,
but I can't help it.

Will I be able to walk and talk?
Will I stay of sound mind?
Will I be able to feed myself?

Will I be alone?

Will I be an autumn leaf,
glorious in color?
Will I be drab and dull,
marred by insects,
mottled with disease?
What kind of leaf will I be?

I want to be happy and sociable,
gracious and thoughtful.
Will disease turn me crotchety and blaming?

I think now I will find friends
and companionship.
How I will think then? I don't know.

I still have the habit
of thinking in the future:
in five years, I will do this,
I will do that.
Someday, I will travel,
write letters, visit people.

I say to myself, "Stop that.
There is no better time than now.
Especially with Parkinson's."

My attitudes must change.
Now I must judge:
Is this money for the spending?
Is it still the time for saving?
What am I saving for?

Is it time that I am hoarding?
Time that's passing through my fingers?
Will I regret I haven't given it away?
Or will I say I frittered it away?

Parkinson's or not—
the questions are the same,
with no right answers.

God's eyes are upon
the ways of mortals,
and he sees all their
steps.
—Job 34:21, adapted

Let the disabled

cast stones into the pond

and note that the ripples

are no less and no more

than from a stone

cast by the fittest of the fit.

Who Is Disabled?

We all are disabled. Vision or hearing problems? Disabled! High blood pressure, arthritis, heart disease? Disabled! Diabetes, cavities in teeth, overweight, too thin, need hormones? Disabled! Crippled! Deprived of ability or power.

Any list of disabilities could go on and on. A disability can be found for most of us. We are powerless in some area of our lives.

Yes, we must use the term *disabilities* for legal purposes: pension, retirement, social security or insurance. But let us not think of *disabled* as describing ourselves.

Let's focus on abilities. We are all able, having power, skill, or talent in some area. Are we able to laugh, think, walk? Read, eat, smile? Almost everyone has an ability.

Disability and ability focus on the way we were at birth and on circumstances since birth. But we have a will that makes us choosers, or to coin a noun, *ablers*.

Ablers develop abilities. Ablers access the power of the Creator in overcoming disabilities or minimizing them. Some ablers with severe disabilities, through choice become rich, yes, rich in abilities, and some even become rich in things!

Unrealistic? No. Ablers are in touch with themselves. They work around their disabilities, becoming competent and capable in other ways. They become rich in soul, rich in mastery of themselves.

Ablers also become enablers of others. One who supports an alcoholic is a negative enabler. We are talking of one who inspires ability, power, capability in others.

This book shares my experience of being disabled by Parkinson's disease and my personal search for ability. With a little thought, you can translate the struggles with Parkinson's into your own struggles.

As an enabler, I believe life has meaning and purpose, even with disabilities. There is a loving Presence who is the Great Enabler. The world's great people have been sustained by a relationship with this Presence. God is present with us. Only God-with-us could enable us.

In later years, disabilities frequently enter life. The healthiest people will someday face disability unless they meet untimely deaths by accident. As your body ages, what interests and activities can you change into abilities?

Finally, laugh at yourself! The search for ability should be fun and exciting! Most of us are half praying mantis and half hippopotamus! We have a devout, praying part of us, and we have an earthy, homely part. For our mental health, we need to feed the homely part with humor.

A disabled person, an abler, and an enabler—we can be all of these at once. So, in some way, pick up your bed and walk!

Stand up, take your mat and walk.
—John 5:8

The Disabled and the Astilbe

Who is disabled?
We are all disabled:
high blood pressure, arthritis, diabetes,
cavities, overweight, underweight,
needing hormones, needing exercise,
heart disease, poor eyesight,
nearly deaf.
Flawed.

The astilbe!
Delicate and perfect!
Flawed?
Not the beautiful astilbe!
Oh! But I see,
a bug crawls there.
Flawed.

Watch the bug,
and it's flawed.
Watch delicacy,
and it's beautiful.

Our flaws loom large in our eyes!
"First take the log out of your own eye,"
Jesus has told us.
But why be critical?

No.
Enough of looking for flaws.
Let's celebrate beauty!

Oh, the astilbe!
She is a lady, perfect, pure, and white,
tall, feathery plumed, and gracious.
Presiding over my garden
in the summer sun.

**Love one another
deeply from the heart.
—*1 Peter 1:22***

My Friend

She was my childhood friend,
and now she's in a nursing home
with multiple sclerosis.
She's a little older than I, but not much.

Does she remember
how we rolled marbles down the steps?
—played school with her chalkboard,
        headed by a scrolling alphabet?
—played upstairs in the side attics?
—built our secret hideout in the woods?
—played among the woodland flowers?

Does she remember
when she had rheumatic fever
and we read about a boy
who grew a Christmas tree in Shantytown?

She taught me to sing a tune on key,
and to sing alto.
She drilled and drilled our trio by piano
until we knew each note
—no muddling through our parts.

Now she lives at the nurses' commands:
Eat breakfast now, sit up now,
lie down now, eat supper now.
She never dreamed that she'd submit
to someone else's times and whims.
But there she is,
and sometimes glad to be there.

Shantytown!
That story still haunts me.
It dares me to plant a tree,
grow a tree, light up a tree,
anywhere, in my private Shantytown,
making a scene of wonder where I live.

My friend with multiple sclerosis
knows how hard it is to find a tree
or a woodland flower,
something to delight the spirit
in her Shantytown.

**Thank you, my friend,
who did so much for
me. I am grateful.**
—Esther

A True Disabler

Today I heard my longtime friend,
Johnny, say he needs AA
to keep him sober.
Did you make him that way, Lord,
giving him a thirst for alcohol
that threatens to consume his body?
He's disabled,
as clearly as I am with Parkinson's.

I came home
and argued with my husband
about who said what
and whose face looked how.
My mind was full of Johnny.

I don't spend each Thursday night
dealing with my attitudes
just to keep on living.
Johnny does.
Maybe I should, too.

Johnny's story mixed up in my head
with a statistic from TV.
"Eighty percent of the mates
of cancer patients
leave their marriages."

Fear,
stirred up by thoughts of Johnny,
filled my mind:
Will Parkinson's make me lose
my marriage, too?

Fear, the true disabler,
grabbed my hand
and pulled me down.

Later, I met Johnny with his wife.
Reality struck: she is a lovely wife.

God, did you give Johnny this disease?
He thinks you did, and for a reason.
Johnny, who was timid,
has learned to tell his story freely.
In disability, a strength grew.

Why should I worry over marriage?
I can't change my disease at all.

Then I read,
"I AM," says the great I AM.
So I too simply am.

God did not give us
a spirit of cowardice,
but one of power, love,
and self-discipline.
—2 Timothy 1:7, adapted

And Now Blind Dad

Clubfoot, back surgery, lung cancer,
heart attack, carotid artery surgery,
and now blind Dad!

His churning, flippered feet
propelled him through the water,
face up, like an otter in the zoo.
That's the way he swims with half a lung.
Lap after lap, sixty laps a workout,
three nights a week.

On days he didn't swim,
he walked—forty-five hundred miles
from retirement to age seventy-three—
and since then, many miles more.
That's how he recovered from
back surgery, heart attack,
lung cancer, carotid artery surgery—
trained in the cardiac rehab program.

Now, at a trim eighty-two, he's nearly blind.
He walks back and forth for exercise,
watches TV with a binoculars,
signs his name under an Optelec magnifier.
He can't see you if you walk by.
Better speak up, or he won't hear you.
All day he sees, not blackness,
but visual patterns forming, re-forming—
walls grow lush trees in winter
or fill up with squiggles.
Yet, he's cheerful and he smiles.

How hard for Dad to give up driving!
He spent a lifetime with machinery—
a farm equipment dealer—
and never took the car to a garage.
He and Mom would pack the camper,
travel coast to coast, north and south,
video camera on tripod beside him,
to catch scenes ahead, along the way.

How hard for him to give up woodworking!
He used to lavish love upon his children,
wrapped up in polished packages of wood.
In my house, there is—
a chest behind my table,
a walnut bed frame with drawers beneath,
a corner shelf, an end table by my sofa,
two six-foot wooden folding tables,
and a chair of reddish wood,
cherry from our land.
With pride and love,
he gave them all to us for Christmas,
year after year, piece by piece!

Your eye is the lamp of
your body. If your eye
is healthy, your whole
body is full of light.
—*Luke 11:34*

Born with a clubfoot,
Dad wore special shoes
that didn't help.
At last, by going barefoot,
he straightened the foot himself,
but one leg grew
a bit longer than the other.
Doing-it-himself has always been
his way of life.

What can he do,
now that he's blind?
He helps my mom keep house
and he invents—
a way to check tire pressure without sight,
little things to care for him and her.
He cares for cars of my three aunts.
He listens to tapes
and practices on a musical keyboard.
He still volunteers
at a church-owned secondhand store.
Doing-for-others has always been
his way of life.

Now Dad walks in blindness
toward the light where stands the Potter.
His feet of clay make tracks upon the snow.
The old is smashed; a new form grows—
one we don't know, chosen by the Potter.
And the Master Potter whispers to the clay
about the role he has in mind for him.

I think: *My clay is strong;*
I walk unaided.
Then one day, I notice
I've been walking
in Dad's steps.

Proclaim the mighty
acts of him who called
you out of darkness
into his marvelous light.
—*1 Peter 2:9*

About Others

She shouldn't have this disease, Lord.
She should have had the polio vaccine.
A bit of carelessness,
and her life is gone,
   gone,
     gone.
She's in a wheelchair all the time,
with a catheter leaking into a plastic bag,
only eighteen years old.
She could have been my child.
I could have been the one
who skipped the vaccine.
Thank you, Lord, I wasn't.

Nathan walks on crutches,
choosing a harder way
of getting around.
No wheelchair for him.
His arms and shoulders are
muscular and strong.
He earns his livelihood,
drives a car to work,
and excels at what he does.

Obvious disabilities!
Everyone notices,
yet doesn't notice after a time.
Who can pity happiness?

Carolyn plays the guitar
and writes music.
She has a heart defect,
had open-heart surgery,
and now must be careful.
Her life may end abruptly.
But she sings the praises of the Lord
for giving her a life and a marriage.

Won't you make it easier for them, Lord?
Give them medical miracles?
Send new technology to help?

The Lord says,
"You are my hands.
What can you do?"

We can all do much
to make this world
a more friendly place
for the disabled.

Treasure of My Heart

She was born with a cleft palate and lip,
this treasure of my heart,
my oldest daughter, Renatta.

She is disabled, but oh, she is able!
Beautiful lady with dark skin and eyes,
groomed to perfection,
she is a beautician, a wife,
a mother of two.

She was born in Cheverly, Maryland,
a city hospital with many babies.
She had to stay there
for her lip to be repaired.
Not till she weighed eight pounds
would they redesign her lip.
So I came home without my baby,
came home without a part of my body.

Then my darling caught an infection,
and the doctor said,
"Don't expect her to live."
When I went to visit,
I stood outside the nursery
where she lay with fifty other babies,
longing to touch and hold,
but lacking permission.
They didn't want her to be contaminated
with the germs from outside the nursery.

I will always be grateful to a Thai nurse
who loved and rocked my baby
on her lunch break.

After two months,
the doctor said,
"She still doesn't weigh eight pounds,
and she still has an infection,
but we're going to do the surgery."

Three days after surgery, she came home.
I resolved that she would not be disabled.
I cuddled her, but not too much.
I spoke clearly so she could imitate.
When the time came for speech therapy,
I was told, "She doesn't need it."

Renatta had more surgeries as she grew older.
It was heartbreaking to hear her cries
when I left her alone in the hospital.
Now hospitals recognize children's emotions, too.

How I wish she were little, to cuddle again,
this treasure of my heart!

> **I, too, was . . . tenderly
> loved by my mother.**
> —*Proverbs 4:3, LB*

Of Two Minds

This crock, when right side up,
looks perfect for mixing punch,
making homemade root beer,
or soaking pickles in brine.
Fine appearance! Don't look inside.

This hour I think,
Why am I taking disability?
I could be working. I feel fine.
Fine appearance!
It is hard to imagine times
when I don't feel fine.
I feel guilty for taking disability.

This hour I am stiff.
Now I remember well
how I felt last year at school,
sitting down to stop the pain
in my back and hips, thinking,
How will I get through the next hour?
wanting to let my mind and body rest,
to lie down in peace,
I didn't let anyone know how I felt inside.
Fine appearance!

"Keep your stresses low," said my doctor.
No one else is aware of my stress.
I seem calm since my pallidotomy.
I no longer shake.
Fine appearance!

This crock is good for something.
To hold kindling beside a fireplace,
to hold pinecones, or yarn for knitting.

Shall I turn this crock upside down,
put a cushion on it,
and use it for a stool?
Everyone will say,
"What a great seat!"
No one will know it has a crack in it.
It will have a
fine appearance!

Two pills and a few hours
stand between
mobility and immobility,
shaking and not shaking.
Without pills, I'd make
no appearance at my job!

Yes, losing a job hurts.
Find other useful things
to do. Hold onto your
God-given self-esteem.

People say, "You look wonderful!"
"If I looked as good
as you look at your age . . ."
"Thank you," I say.
I like to be upbeat and positive!

Now this matter of my disability
is forcing me to tell the truth.
"How are you?" someone asks.
For years I said, "Fine, thank you."
Shall I tell the truth? "I am in pain.
I can hardly stand so long."

With planning and time,
I can do many things.
I could teach every day
if the students would wait
for me to eat when I am hungry,
if the students would wait
for me to rest,
if the students would wait
for my pills to work when I am stiff.
But the students can't wait.

One day, I knew:
The time has come to take disability.
I am tired of keeping up appearances.
I know what I am.
It is up to me to keep my stresses low.
I must be true to what I know is best.

Others may take my place in the light.
I will retire to the shadows.
To use a parachute, one has to jump.
But oh, how scary!
Taking disability is scary.
To leave my job, financial security!
I will write, but through writing,
I have never earned much.

Now, if you ask me how I am,
I don't know what I'll say
because I am of two minds.
I am aware of disability and ability.
I could answer you from disability,
but I probably won't.
I'll probably say, "I'm fine!"
because I *am* fine,
and it's a beautiful day to be alive!

When people ask,
"How are you?"
do they really want
to know?

Bird on a Nest

Carolina wren sits in moss and dried flowers.
Black eyes alert, day after day.
Watching, waiting, watching, waiting.
My camera lens confronts her.
She sits still, still, still. Click. Still.
She is afraid but
she has priorities.
Fear isn't one of them.

I go about my life, day after day.
People talk, but I go on.
Working, thinking, watching, waiting.
Taking written snapshots of our lives.
I am afraid, but I can't give in to fear.
I have my priorities.
Fear isn't one of them.

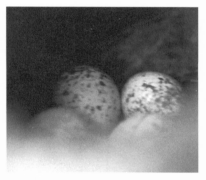

They say I look normal now.
I've had a pallidotomy.
How long it lasts,
I do not know. No one knows.
I have faced a monster
breathing immobility.
I've come back
and found that life's too precious
to care what others think.

You see,
I have these eggs to hatch.
A hundred books to write.

**Spend the rest of your
life doing what you
truly want to do.**

*T*here comes a day

when one realizes

that living with disease successfully

is in the mastery

of many details.

Cups on Saucers

Two cups on two saucers,
crowded together.
Clattering, chattering, friendly cups.

Two people talking,
crowded together.
Sociable, chatting, friendly folks.

The chime of pottery touching pottery.
Cups cannot chime alone.

The pleasure of person meeting person,
exciting laughter in both!

Chiming, ringing, tinkling pottery!
Laughing, loving, singing people!

Spoon taps on cup,
the pottery rings!
Cup to my lips,
the tea steams and stings.
Ah, let me not sip alone.
Give me instead two cups of tea,
one for you and one for me.
Good for the heart and the spirit!

I talk about me
in my shaky condition.
That leaves you free
to comment and question.
Good for the heart and the spirit!

We share this tea.
Thanks, my friend.
Communion of laughter or tears.
I listen, you talk.
You share situations.
You need to hear that I care.

And so, we joke
of mutual concerns,
but sometimes,
fear drips in our cups.

Ah, tea for two, or four, or six!
This drinking of tea
is enabling me
to stay in touch with humanity!
Good for the heart and the spirit!

**Laugh at yourself!
Talk about your
disease. Then others
will feel comfortable
with you.**

Telling a Beech by Its Bark

Silvery gray, smooth, streaked with black: A beech!
I can tell a beech by its bark.
Parkinson's! These are my symptoms,
these my bark:

*S*haking, the most visible of signs.
   *S*tiffness, quite debilitating.
      *S*lowness: "Hurry up," they say.
     *S*tooping, painful every day.

*S*huffling makes me look so old.
   *S*taring, with eyes fixed and cold.
     *S*peechless, tongue-tied.

Writing *small* upon the page,
sometimes barely read at all.
*S*tanding *s*till, a concrete statue,
helpless, frozen to the floor.

My *s*ingle-*s*ided symptoms *s*preading
right side first, and then to left.
Symptoms joined to make a syndrome,
symptoms starting all with *S*.

These are my symptoms, just for me.
What are your symptoms? What, your bark?
Someday you may need to know.
Make a list, keep a medical diary.

You may need to know
   for insurance,
   for a doctor,
   for retirement,
   for disability,
   for social security,
   for genealogy records,
   for research,
   for future medical treatment,
   for personal knowledge,
   for your children
   and their children,
   who may want to know
   their chance of inheriting
   your disease.

Keep daily diaries of medications and their doses; when they reach peak levels; how one feels at peak levels; how severe the "off" times are; at what time as well as what types and amounts of food and/or liquids are ingested; plus any other comments that might help establish a pattern. From these patterns, doctors can more personally titrate medications and their schedules. —*Thomas R. Kelly, in* UPF Newsletter, *1998, no. 3.*

Make entries in your medical diary as changes come in your condition.

Trimming the Plates

Lord, trim this plate!
I can't do it myself.

I'm overweight.
I need help.
Trim the plate!

I don't eat too much in the morning.
I don't eat too much at noon.
But, when evening has come,
and I'm idle and social,
I'm tempted.
Oh, Lord, trim this plate!

I don't want my arteries
filled with fat and debris.
I don't want heart disease or angina.
But cholesterol is high
and my willpower's low.
I'm tempted.
Oh, Lord, trim this plate!

So I'll try this technique
of delay and eat.
Of course, I can eat, but not yet.
If I delay, stretch the time before eating,
then the food should pile up,
somewhere in the future.
A trick of the mind!
Who cares why it works?

The real problem is, Lord,
I don't eat what I ought.
I don't eat my veggies, but cake.
So cholesterol's high
and my willpower's low.
I'm tempted.
Oh, Lord, trim this plate!

**God will dwell
in the temple
you give him.**

Day Moon

Day moon,
pale white circle
in the autumn sky,
pill for the earth to swallow.
Day moon,
you remind me of my pills.
Again I forgot to take them.

Do I not care enough
about my body
to remember?
Yes, I care.
Then I must set up
some way to remember.

I ask for help:
"Lord, my pills!
I keep forgetting.
How can I think to take them?"

Set an alarm?
Get a digital pillbox with a countdown timer?
Post my medication schedule?
Fill a daily pillbox with my pills?
Keep a diary of medications?
Put my morning pills beside my bed?
Carry an emergency supply in my pocketbook?
Leave an extra set of pills at work?
Count them out the night before?
Or do several of these?

There has to be an answer
to fit my personality.
I'll settle on a system
and keep on following it,
till it is second nature.

I count pills for each day
and tote a backup supply.
There! That's better!
I do remember.
I can tell when I've forgotten:
I've already doled out the doses.

**Develop a way
to remember
medication. Then
make it into a habit.**

Inchworm

I watched an inchworm
lift its head
and sway its body right and left
and up and down.
It exercised!
I don't think it had arthritis!

Arthritis?
Do inchworms get arthritis?
If every joint were painful when he bends,
would he still loop along?

Right and left and up and down,
so I must move,
in spite of painful joints.

I saw an inchworm sitting in a loop.
How long could it sit so
without losing strength
and range of motion?

What I would be, I must begin.
If I'd be agile, I must stretch and bend.
If feet won't work, then hands must move!
If arms won't work, then legs!
Every body part that functions
has need of movement,
movement, vital movement.

Vital for the heart and circulation.
Vital for all the body's functions.
Vital to retard the aging process.

Let me move like an inchworm,
slow and steady, on and on.
Or will I be an inchworm
which has ceased to move?
A shriveled bit of green?

**Move any body part
you can. Movement
will retard the aging
process.**

Princess

My granddaughter, this small princess:
What shall I tell her about my disease,
appropriate for her age?
No tears. No mournful voice.

To babies:
"I'm a shaky Grandma!" and laugh!

To young children:
"I'm shaky and stiff!
That's the way your Grandma is!"

To older children:
"The doctor said I have Parkinson's.
It makes me shaky and stiff.
You won't get it from me,
and I won't die from it."
(Children worry about
themselves and death.
Reassure them so they don't need to ask.)

More comments as needed:
"My brain doesn't make enough dopamine.
Dopamine sends messages in our brains
    to make our bodies move."
"I am not feeling mean.
    My face is stuck!"

Whatever the disease,
be prepared for an older child's anger
    and embarrassment.

Make a rule:
"You may tell me I'm a messy eater,
that I'm gross, that I take baby steps,
that I'm an embarrassment—
anything at all in private,
but never in public."
(What I permit will become the way
my child will treat others.)

Give others patience, acceptance,
love, and care.
My disease is my chance to teach.

Tell the truth about your disease as fits the age. If you don't, the child may imagine the worst.

Duck Questions

Where did you get those markings, little duck?
From your mother or your father,
or are they painted on?
Will knowing make your black feet white?

Where did I get this disease?
From inheritance or from environment?
What does it matter?

Is my Parkinson's from brain injury?
A horse kicked me in the head.
(In 1817, James Parkinson blamed injury!)
From poisons?
I've been exposed to pesticides and herbicides.
(In 1817, Parkinson blamed noxious exposure!)
Or is this idiopathic, without known cause?
A disease process set in motion by genetics?

Why should you care?
Parkinson's is rare before age fifty,
increases in frequency with age.
You may yet get Parkinson's.
Most surely someone in your family will.

Why should we care?
Whatever our disease or disability,
we have power to help find answers
and thus, we hope, the cure.

These things I can do
because I care:
• donate my brains and body
  to research at my death.
• take part in studies seeking answers
  to heredity and environment.
• take part in drug trials.
• take part in surgical trials.
• promote understanding of the disease.

**Don't just ask, "Why?"
Do something about it!
Contribute in life or in
death, or both!**

Beyond disabilities

lie the treasures of God,

given through his Spirit

to those humble enough

to give up

their preconceived beliefs.

Ice Sculpture

The Master has been sculpting
in the night.
I heard the tools he used:
the wind and freezing rain.

Had I not seen,
my mind would not conceive
the wending path of ice
through forest.
There is no stream here,
no pathway,
nothing that would lead the mind
to dream of stream of ice.
Yet here it is,
and it's been given
but for an hour or two.
Not twice.

The Master has been sculpting
in the night.
The tools he used:
my dreams and deep desires.

Had he not sent the dream,
my mind would not conceive
the scenes I saw.

Pray every night for dreams!
Then be prepared
for wending path of dreams
that leads you on.

The guiding dream for many days,
or years, may last
but for an hour or two
and then be gone.

The Master has been sculpting
in the night.
The dream is clear.
Dare we believe the dream?
Are we afraid to follow?

**Ask God for a vision
of his best plan
for you.**

The Lid's On

"I will give you treasures
hidden in the darkness,
secret riches;
and you will know
that I am doing this."
　(Isaiah 45:3, LB)

What treasure is within this jar,
hidden in the darkness?
Secret riches?
Oh, I would be rich.

Secret riches.
What riches do I want?
What riches can you give me?
Money? Health? Love? Time?
Or perhaps peace of mind?

Money: the medium of exchange.
Money for things?
Money for health?
May I exchange it for love?
Can I buy peace of mind?

Or could the secret riches be health?
If I had health, I could work for money.
I would be more attractive.
I wouldn't worry as much,
so I think!

I think! Are these the magic words
that take off the lid?
Will thinking give me riches?

Think! To pray is to think.
In prayer, we visualize and verbalize
our deepest wishes and desires.
In prayer, we create electrical impulses.
Like messages from a distant satellite,
the beeping of a space station far distant,
our thoughts go out to God.

Think! But do not limit God.
Wait in humble anticipation
of what God has hidden in the jar.
"God is able to accomplish
abundantly far more
than all we can ask or imagine."
　(Ephesians 3:20, adapted)

**Recognize the treasure
God has given you.
Be thankful!**

The Spinning Wheel

I keep spinning around and around,
thinking the same things over again,
saying the same things,
writing and doing the same things.
I want to be creative.
I need a new vision.

The threads of my life
slide through my fingers.
I sit here, day after day,
spinning, spinning, spinning,
with plenty of time to pray,
but not praying,
until I am dry and brittle
as flax in drought.

Then, nearly lifeless,
I beg, " Spirit,
plead for me."
Spirit! The source of new thoughts.
But I don't know what I need.

There is a rustling in the flax
as new juices flow
from the roots upward,
making the threads pliable again.
Now there is flax for the spinning,
as my great-great-grandmother spun it.

There is a rustling in the spirit
as new thoughts flow.
Here at my spinning wheel,
sitting at the same spot,
I travel through time and space,
journey toward ideas and accomplishment,
and revel in the richness of emotion.

"The Spirit helps us in our weakness;
for we do not know how to pray as we ought,
but that very Spirit intercedes with sighs
    too deep for words.
And God, who searches the heart,
knows what is the mind of the Spirit,
because the Spirit intercedes for the saints
according to the will of God."
    (Romans 8:26-27)

**What is impossible
for mortals is possible
for God.**
—Luke 18:27

When I Think I Know the Answers

A potter forms his clay
upon the wheel
from bottom up:
Deduction I have made
from watching him.
I think I know his way.
And then he takes the clay,
without a bottom,
fits a lid.
My thinking is upset.
Just when I think I know the answers,
I'm startled with thoughts
I've never thought before.

When Paul and Silas were in jail,
a midnight earthquake broke their bonds.
They didn't flee like others would.
They stayed: that was their mission.
When the jailer saw them there,
he asked what to do to be saved.

They promised him and his house
salvation by believing.
So gathered all to hear the news of Christ,
the gospel to believe,
baptism to receive.

Paul and Silas didn't say,
"We'll have to wait for day
to think things over and find a river.
Into what church will you be baptized?
Don't decide in heat of strong emotion.

This is too sudden to be really true.
These youths and servants in commotion,
have they received the church instruction?
How can they understand baptism?
Are we sure these folks believe?
To save their skin, do they deceive?"

The jailer asked prisoners Paul and Silas,
" 'Sirs, what must I do to be saved?'
They answered, 'Believe on the Lord Jesus,
and you will be saved,
you and your household.'
They spoke the word of the Lord to him
and to all who were in his house.
At the same hour of the night
he took them and washed their wounds;
then he and his entire family were baptized
without delay."
   (Acts 16:30-33)

The dimensions of
thought will be
constantly changing
as long as we live.

Candle Pots

To some is given a special task
to be a candle pot,
with holes releasing light.

Luminous, their personalities.
Tender, their emotions.
Courageous, their dispositions.
Electric, their thoughts.
Humble, their beliefs.

Power is in their possession,
all the spiritual power
they will ever need.

Forgetting things behind
and reaching for the future,
every night once more,
they drop that day into the past.
The Light they accept as a gift
and give it away with love.
Its flame is never consumed,
but brighter glows as years pass by.

To be a candle pot requires
that holes be cut into the clay.
One must surrender
to the Potter
and to the cutting of the wire.

Sometimes I wish that I were
a candle pot,
or a pitcher that pours out joy,
or another kind of pot
with a different purpose.
But, no, I will drop crumbs,
the occupation given me.

"No eye has seen, nor ear heard,
nor the human heart conceived,
what God has prepared
for those who love him."
    (1 Corinthians 2:9)

To all who received him,
who believed in his
name, he gave power.
—John 1:12

*T*he door to success

is marked PUSH.

All must push.

How is up to you.

(Fax numbers labeled • Web sites: http://www.— • Internet E-mail: —@—)

Patients Taking Part in Parkinson's Research

- Columbia Presbyterian Medical Center. Studies role of genetics in Parkinson's disease. Call if there are two or more living people with PD within a family: 212-305-5779.
- Genzyme Genetics. Baylor DNA Diagnostic Laboratory. For about $150, have your DNA stored for future studies: 800-255-7357 or 800-226-3624.
- Ohio State University Parkinson's Disease Center of Excellence. Genetic and epidemiological research programs: 614-688-4808.
- Parkinson's Disease Foundation. Gives patient referrals for treatment and information on brain donors: 800-457-6676.

Associations and Foundations for Parkinson's

- American Academy of Neurology. 1080 Montreal Ave., St. Paul, MN 55116. Gives abstracts of research into Alzheimer's, Parkinson's, strokes, and migraines. 612-683-1940. www.aan.com
- American Parkinson's Disease Association, Suite 4B, 1250 Hylan Blvd., Staten Island, NY 10305. Nationwide grassroots organization that funds research and offers assistance to patients and families through support and education. 800-223-2732. www.apdaparkinson.com and apda@admin.con2.com
- National Institute of Neurological Disorders and Stroke, Office of Scientific Health Reports, P.O. Box 5801, Bethesda, MD 20824. www.ninds.nih.gov
- National Parkinson's Foundation, 1501 NW 9th Ave. & Bob Hope Road, Miami, FL 33136. International organization that funds research, supports researchers, provides diagnostic and therapeutic services, organizes support groups and conferences, and provides educational materials and services. Provides names of 51 medical Centers of Excellence in the USA and abroad. Publication: *Parkinson Report.* 800-327-4545 or 800-433-7022. www.parkinson.org and mailbox@npf.med.miami.edu
- PDF-UPF is one organization maintaining two addresses and publishing *Parkinson's Disease Foundation Newsletter.*

  Parkinson's Disease Foundation, 710 West 168th St., 3rd Floor, New York, NY 10032-9982. 800-457-6676. www.pdf.org

  United Parkinson Foundation, 833 W. Washington Blvd., Chicago, IL 60607. Funds and supports research, sponsors symposia, promotes support groups, provides patient services and educational materials, and publishes news of recent events. 312-733-1893.
- Parkinson's Foundation of Canada, Suite 710, 390 Bay St., Toronto, ON M5H 2Y2, Canada: 800-565-3000. www.parkinson.ca and sarah.hoddinott@parkinson.ca
- Young Parkinson's Support Network of California. APDA Young Parkinson's R & I Center, 1041 Foxenwood Dr., Santa Maria, CA 93455. Gives referrals to other support groups: 800-223-9776.

Information on Parkinson's

- *Capital Chapter News.* Published by Capital Chapter of NPF: 202-466-0550. www.parkinson.org
- New York Online Access to Health (NOAH): www.noah.cuny.edu/Neurological Disorders
- Parkinson's Disease: *Doctor's Guide to the Internet.* Published online by National Library of Medicine.

Offers MEDLINE on the Internet. Accesses archives of abstracts related to Parkinson's Disease. Has up-to-date and technical information for doctors and patients, with many links: www.pslgroup.com/PARKINSON.HTM
- "Parkinson's Disease Support" can be searched on the Internet. A resource list of organizations concerned about Parkinson's: http://132.183.175.10:80/./PD-SUPRT.HTM
- *Parkinson's Disease Update*. Published by Medical Publishing Co., PO Box 450, Huntingdon Valley, PA 19006. Eight-page monthly newsletter, by subscription. Reports on newest knowledge and treatment: 215-947-6648. Fax: 215-947-2252.
- *PROPATH*. 525 Middlefield Rd., Suite 250, Menlo Park, CA 94025. Funded by a grant from Sandoz Pharmaceuticals Corporation. A series of booklets and questionnaires with practical suggestions on managing Parkinson's disease; available through physicians. Publishes a *Bibliography Booklet*. 415-324-0500.

Patient Support and/or Information Groups

Access Center for Independent Living: 937-341-5202. www.acil.com

Al-Anon Family Group Public Information Hotline: 800-344-2666

Alcoholics Anonymous World Services: 212-870-3400. Check local phone directory for AA, Al-Anon, and Alateen. www.alcoholics-anonymous.org (English, Spanish, French)

Alzheimer's Disease Association: 800-621-0379

American Academy of Neurology: www.aan.com

American Association of Kidney Patients: 800-749-2257

American Burn Association: 800-548-2876

American Diabetes Association: 800-232-3472

American Liver Foundation, Hepatitis Liver Disease Hotline: 800-223-0179

American Printing House for the Blind, free tours, educ. aids for visually impaired: www.aph.org

American Trauma Society: 800-556-7890

Amyotrophic Lateral Sclerosis Association, Info and Referral Service: 800-782-4747

Association for Cerebral Palsy: 800-639-1930

Asthma and Allergy Foundation of America Information Line: 800-7ASTHMA

Better Hearing Institute, a charitable organization not selling products: 800-327-9355

Candlelighters Childhood Cancer Foundation: 800-366-2223

Central Autonomic Disorders, Natl. Dysautonomia Res. Foundation: www.ndrf.org/central.htm

Children's Hospice International; founded, directed by Ann Armstrong-Dailey: 800-242-4453

Cleft Palate Foundation: 800-242-5338

Cleveland Sight Center: 216-791-8118. www.clevesight.org

Coast to Coast Disability and National Resource Directory: www.coast-resource.com

Deafness Research Foundation: 800-535-3323 = 800-535-DEAF

Epilepsy Foundation of America Information Center: 800-332-1000

Lupus Foundation of America Information Hotline: 800-558-0121

Multiple Sclerosis Foundation: 800-441-7055. www.msfacts.org

Multiple Sclerosis Society of Canada: 410-922-6065

Myasthenia Gravis Foundation: 800-541-5454

National AIDS Hotline: 800-342-2437

National Association for the Dually Diagnosed: 800-331-5362

National Association for the Visually Handicapped, with on-line store at 22 W. 21st ST., New York, NY 10010: 212-889-3141. www.navh.org

National Center for Youth with Disability: 800-729-6686

National Down's Syndrome Society: 800-221-4602

National Drug Treatment Referral and Information Hotline: 800-378-4435 and 800-DRU-HELP

National Easter Seal Society: 800-221-6827

National Headache Foundation: 800-843-2256

National Head Injury Foundation: 800-444-6443

National Hospice Organization: 800-658-8898

National Institute of Neurological Disorders and Stroke: www.ninds.nih.gov/Health Information/ Parkinson's

National Library of Medicine MEDLINE: www.med-portal.com/PubMed

National Lymphedema Network: 800-541-3259

National Mental Health Association: 800-969-6642

National Multiple Sclerosis Society, Chicago-Greater IL: 800-FIGHT-MS. www.ncc.nmsis.org

National Neurofibromatosis Foundation: 800-323-7938

National Organization for Rare Disorders: 800-999-6673

National Spinal Cord Injury Association: 800-962-9629

National Tuberous Sclerosis Association: 800-225-6872

Office of Cancer Communications: 800-422-6237

REDI: Recycled Equipment Donated for Independence, Dayton, Ohio: 937-341-5218

Society for the Blind, 2750 24th St., Sacramento, CA 95818-3299: 916-452-8271

Spina Bifida Association of America: 800-621-3141

Stiff Man Syndrome Foundation: stiffman-requests@lists.zyx.net

Stuttering Foundation of America: 800-992-9392

Technical Aids and Assistance for the Disabled Center: 800-346-2939 (Illinois only), or 312-421-3373.

tadd@interaccess.com

United Cerebral Palsy Associations: 800-872-5827

United Leukodystrophy Foundation: 800-728-5483

Visiting Nurse Association of America: 888-866-8773

Searching the Internet

If no organization is found here for your disability, find a friend with Internet access. There is plenty of information about any health subject on the Internet. There are also chatrooms where patients may find each other and give support.

Internet addresses change frequently, so don't assume your organization is no longer on the Internet. Try a search with the name.

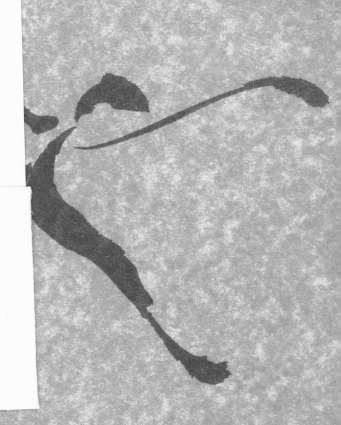